The end of Kate's bed was a lonely place.

Tiger the cat no longer slept there. Tiger died last winter,

so there were only Kate's two feet to keep each other company.

Now Kate woke to Full Summer with the sun pouring

over the back fence...

For Carolyn,
Rosy and Sasha

First published 2001 by Walker Books Ltd
87 Vauxhall Walk, London SE11 5HJ

This edition published 2007

10 9 8 7 6 5 4

This book has been typeset in Bulmer MT

Printed in China

British Library Cataloguing in Publication Data:
a catalogue record for this book is available from the British Library

ISBN 978-1-4063-0851-8

www.walker.co.uk

WALKER BOOKS
AND SUBSIDIARIES

LONDON • BOSTON • SYDNEY • AUCKLAND

"Let's Get a PUP!"

Bob Graham

"Let's get a pup!" said Kate.

"What, a brand-new one?"
said a now wide-awake Mum.
"With the wrapping still on?"
added her breathless dad.
"Pups don't come wrapped,"
replied Kate.
"I know they don't," said Dad.
"It's just a joke."

Mum looked in the paper.

"It must be small," said Kate.

"And cute," said Dad.

"And get all excited," said Kate.

"And run round in circles," said Dad.

"Hmm," said Mum. "LOOK!"

THE RESCUE CENTRE
The centre for dogs without a home
The centre for dogs all alone

With their breakfast uneaten,
they dressed and left immediately.

At the Rescue Centre they found plenty of dogs
without a home, and lots of dogs all alone. They found …

big dogs, small dogs, sniffers and sleepers,
wire-haireds, short-haireds, scratchers and leapers.

They found fighters and biters, growlers and snarlers, short dogs,
dogs long and thin, and dogs with their cheeks sucked in.

They also found happy dogs, sad dogs,
"take me" dogs, and dogs who couldn't care less.

They saw smelly dogs, fat dogs,

   lean and mean dogs, chew-it-up-

     and-spit-it-out-at-you dogs,

      and dogs like walking nightmares.

        Then they saw ...

Dave.

Dave was so excited
he came out sideways.
He barked twice,
water flew off his tongue
and he turned a complete
circle in the air.

He was small.
He was cute.
He was brand-new.

Dave climbed right
over the top of Kate,
who briefly
wore him
like a hat.

"He's all that we want," said Kate.

"All that we came for," said Mum.

"We'll take him,"
  said Dad.

Then they saw …

Rosy.

And she saw them.

She was old and grey and broad as a table.

It was difficult for her to get to her feet,

but she stood, it seemed, almost politely.

Her eyes watered, her ears went back

and she radiated Good Intention.

"My wish for you," said Dad,

"is that you could lie on someone's

living-room floor."

"Or on their couch," said Mum.

"Or on someone's bed," said Kate.

Mum's voice shook.

"We would take them all if we could,

but what can we do?"

And with many a backward glance ...

they slowly walked away.

At home, Dave was everything
that a pup could be,
and more.

On his first night, he cried in his carton.

The next morning, Kate's mum and dad
received a good licking.

"Dave was crying last night, so he slept with me,"
said Kate. "But I didn't sleep…"

"Neither did I," said Dad. "I was wishing…"

"Neither did I," said Mum. "I was wishing…"

With their breakfast once again
uneaten, they dressed
and left immediately.

At the Rescuc Centre
Rosy was waiting for them.

"Let's get you home," said Dad.

Rosy was instantly at home.
Her broad heavy tail swept everything
off the low table.

"I've seen a dog smelling a man,
   but never a man smelling a dog,"
   said Kate's mum.
"She needs a bath," said Dad.

Now Dad's wish has come true.

Rosy is asleep on the living-room floor,

with Dave to keep her company.

Mum's wish has also come true.

Now Rosy and Dave are asleep on the couch.

And what of Kate's wish?

Will it come true as well?

Yes.

Dave and Rosy
will get to sleep
on someone's bed.

Kate puts her head on
Rosy's stomach.
She hears angry gurgles,
squeaks and plops,
lonely corkscrew sounds,
and the pump, pump, pump
of Rosy's heart, like a
big hollow engine room.

Kate's feet are no longer lonely under the blankets.

It seems like Dave and Rosy have always been there.

Their weight is comfortable and reliable, and will stop

Kate's bed floating away into the night.